Topic: Kindergarten and Friends **Subtopic:** School Supplies/ Things in t...

Notes to Parents and Teachers:

As a child becomes more familiar reading books, it is important for him/her to rely on and use reading strategies more independently to help figure out words they do not know.

REMEMBER: PRAISE IS A GREAT MOTIVATOR!

Here are some praise points for beginning readers:

• I saw you get your mouth ready to say the first letter of that word.

• I like the way you used the picture to help you figure out that word.

• I noticed that you saw some sight words you knew how to read!

Book Ends for the Reader!

Here are some reminders before reading the text:

• Point to each word you read to make it match what you say.

• Use the picture for help.

• Look at and say the first letter sound of the word.

• Look for sight words that you know how to read in the story.

• Think about the story to see what word might make sense.

Words to Know Before You Read

bag

crayons

cupboard

eraser

pencil

pocket

teacher

Is it in my bag?

No! Where is my eraser?

Is it in the cupboard?

No! Where is my eraser?

Is it in my pocket?

No! But there is candy in my pocket.

Does the teacher have it?

No! Where is my eraser?

Is it in my pencil case?

No! But my crayons are.

What do I do? I'll ask Anna.

Do you have my eraser?

No, I don't!

Wait a minute!

There is my eraser!

It is in my shirt pocket!

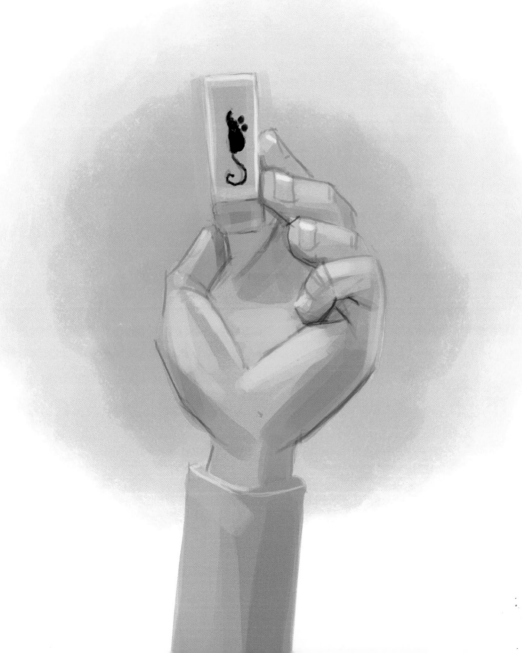

I found it. Hooray!

Book Ends for the Reader

I know...

1. What is the boy looking for in the story?

2. Where did he look to find his eraser?

3. Where was his eraser?

I think ...

1. Have you ever lost something?

2. Who did you ask to help you find it?

3. How did you find it?

Book Ends for the Reader

What happened in this book?

Look at each picture and talk about what happened in the story.

About the Author

Robert Rosen lives in South Korea with his wife, son and dog. He has taught kindergarten and elementary students since 2010. He likes to travel the world riding new roller coasters.

About the Illustrator

Marcin Piwowarski is self-taught in traditional as well as digital illustration. Marcin managed to make over one thousand books during his twenty-year artistic journey. As a single father of three kids, he understands what to include in his art for it to be adored and eye-catching.

Library of Congress PCN Data

Where is My Eraser? / Robert Rosen

ISBN 978-1-68342-710-0 (hard cover)(alk.paper)
ISBN 978-1-68342-762-9 (soft cover)
ISBN 978-1-68342-814-5 (e-Book)
Library of Congress Control Number: 2017935355

Rourke Educational Media
Printed in the United States of America, North Mankato, Minnesota

© 2018 Rourke Educational Media

www.rourkeeducationalmedia.com

Edited by: Debra Ankiel
Art direction and layout by: Rhea Magaro-Wallace
Cover and interior Illustrations by: Marcin Piwowarski